W9-CTT-263

Illustrated by Jerrod Maruyama

Customer Service: 1-877-277-9441 or customerservice@pikidsmedia.com

Published by Phoenix International Publications, Inc.
8501 West Higgins Road   59 Gloucester Place
Chicago, Illinois 60631   London W1U 8JJ

PI Kids and *we make books come alive* are trademarks of
Phoenix International Publications, Inc., and are registered
in the United States.

www.pikidsmedia.com

8 7 6 5 4 3 2 1

ISBN: 978-1-   5441-6

Disney

My First Stories

ALICE WANTS TO GROW

we make books come alive®

pi kids **Phoenix International Publications, Inc.**

Chicago • London • New York • Hamburg • Mexico City • Sydney

Alice sees a bottle that says DRINK ME and a cake that says EAT ME.
"Which one should I try?" she asks.

Just then, the Cheshire Cat appears. "The drink will make you shrink, and the cake will make you grow. So, do you want to be big, or do you want to be small?" he asks.

Alice stops to think. "When I'm small, I can squeeze into tiny spaces for hide-and-seek."

"Did she go this way?" Tweedledee asks.

"Or that way?" asks Tweedledum.

"When I'm big, I can reach a shelf up high," Alice says.

"Would you get that teapot for me, please?" the little mouse asks.

"Of course!" Alice replies.

"When I'm small, I can crawl under things," says Alice, "like this mushroom."

"This is my mushroom," says the Caterpillar grumpily.

"But there's enough mushroom for both of us!" Alice says.

"When I'm big, I can reach the Doorknob and turn it all by myself," says Alice. "May I come in?"

"Yes!" says the Doorknob. "Just be gentle with my nose, please."

"When we're small, we hold hands, so we don't lose each other," says Alice.
"This way to the croquet court!" says the Queen of Hearts.

"When I'm big, I can walk alone," says Alice. "And I can go in any direction I choose."

TEA
PARTY

♥CROQUET
COURT♥

"When I'm small, people tell me stories," says Alice.

"I know a story about a walrus," the Mad Hatter says. "Would you like to hear it?"

"Yes, please!" Alice says, and she claps her hands.

"When I'm big, I can read to myself," says Alice. "I like to take my books outside with my kitty cat."

"When I'm small, I can't run very fast," says Alice.

"But we can!" say the hedgehogs. "Hurry up!"

"When I'm big, I can catch up with the White Rabbit. Wait for me!" says Alice. "Why are you always in such a hurry?"

"I'm late for a tea party," says the White Rabbit. "Won't you join me?"

"Hmmm," says Alice. "What size should I be for the tea party?"

"It doesn't really matter," says the White Rabbit, "because big or small, everyone fits right in!"